DATE DUE

12/09

METAMORPHOSIS
Junior Year

METAMORPHOSIS
Junior Year

BETSY FRANCO

drawings by **TOM FRANCO**

CANDLEWICK PRESS

Text copyright © 2009 by Betsy Franco
Illustrations copyright © 2009 by Tom Franco

The lines from "brainy poet" Paula's poem are from "Letter to a John" by
Portia Carryer, who holds all rights; the lines are used here by her permission.
Four of Portia Carryer's poems are included in the anthology, *Falling Hard:
100 Love Poems by Teenagers* (Candlewick Press, 2008).

Mitchell Murdock is the author of *Running Out* and *Heroguy*, attributed
to Duwayne. Mitchell Murdock holds all rights to his graphic novels,
the titles of which are used here by his permission.

A poem, "Ian," similar to the prose passage "Then, somehow it got worse. . . .
So I've gotten as mute as a moth." appeared in my book *Conversations with a Poet:
Inviting Poetry into the K–12 Classroom*
(Richard C. Owen, 2005), page 105.

First edition 2009

Library of Congress Cataloging-in-Publication Data

Franco, Betsy.

Metamorphosis : junior year / Betsy Franco; illustrated by Tom Franco. — 1st ed.

p. cm.

Summary: High school artist Ovid's journal recasts his classmates' lives and loves as
modern-day Roman mythology, while slowly revealing his own struggles with parents who
need him to be the perfect son in the wake of his meth-addicted sister's disappearance.

ISBN 978-0-7636-3765-1

[1. Family problems — Fiction. 2. Artists — Fiction. 3. High schools — Fiction.
4. Schools — Fiction. 5. Emotional problems — Fiction.
6. Mythology, Roman — Fiction. 7. Diaries — Fiction.] I. Franco, Tom, ill. II. Title.

PZ7.F8475Met 2009

[Fic] — dc22   2009013859

2 4 6 8 10 9 7 5 3 1

Printed in the United States of America

This book was typeset in Trump Mediaeval.

Candlewick Press
99 Dover Street
Somerville, Massachusetts 02144

visit us at www.candlewick.com

For Mary Lee Donovan, my editor

fall quarter

is it fate?

prison

So here I am in my room with this notebook I got for drawing, and now I'm writing in it, too. In a desperate attempt to retrieve my sanity from the trash. There better be some god of journals and blogs who cares about what I'm saying, or I'm screwed.

For sure, my parents would die to read this. I wouldn't be surprised if they opened the door any minute. Without knocking.

"How's it going in here? What's that you're writing in?"

Privacy went out the window about six months ago in this house—after the family fell apart. I keep the notebook under my mattress and smooth out the bed. That way, Mom doesn't have any reason to come in to supposedly straighten up, when her real agenda is sniffing, searching, and snooping.

Actually, there's not much to clean up in here. Just the jumble of markers and paintbrushes on my desk that have their own sense of order. A sculpture of a guy made out of masking tape. A few of my tamer sketches tacked to the wall. And my ratty old blue comforter—the one my sister and I used to sit under and have séances.

Last time my best friend Jack came over, he sat on the bed for at most three seconds, rubbing his pitching shoulder.

"Let's get out of here," he said. "Your room's like a cell. All you need is a toilet in the corner."

Interesting that Jack would say that now, when I'm feeling like my house has become a maximum-security prison and my parents are the guards.

If they only knew what they've pushed me to do.

six degrees from normal

School's mostly a relief from home.

On milder days, Mom starts up with: "We just want you to be happy, succeed in life. No one in this family needs to be pulled down by what's happened—least of all, you."

Dad pitches in: "You've got so much potential—a good solid brain, for starters."

But usually their cheery chant revs into a rant: "Don't spend so much time in your room, stop drawing so much, join a club, get normal. Now."

To appease them, I actually started dropping in on a club. I couldn't see myself in Robotics or Yearbook or Spanish Club or Junior Senators or whatever. My poet friend Paula always says she's starting a writing club, but it never happens. So even though I hardly knew the first thing about it, I actually showed up at yoga. Twisting up like a pretzel, touching my head to the floor between my legs, doing handstands—the works.

I did it partly to try to chill out. One positive side effect is that it gets me to breathe—something I've pretty much forgotten how to do. And besides, there's a lot of girls in there. In particular, one very flexible girl whose bare shoulders are the color of mocha coffee.

"You joined a yoga club?" Mom said, with those deep lines between her eyebrows. "Oh, Ovid. That's not remotely the kind of club we had in mind."

She says stuff like that to me. But I don't say the stuff I'd like to say to her. 'Cause it would just go something like this:

"If you're gonna micromanage my life now . . ."

"What in the world do you mean, Ovid?"

"If you're gonna smother the parts of me that remind you of 'she-who-self-destructed,' you're gonna have to think about changing my name."

"You're not making any sense."

"Oh yeah, well, what did you have in mind when you gave me a name like Ovid? You started it. You and Dad basically gave me the green light to go outside the box, and now it's freakin' you out."

"There's absolutely no room for attitude in this family, Ovid. Not anymore. End of subject!"

what's in a name?

Would things be different or better with me now if my parents had given me a normal name? Probably not. My name can't be what's screwing me up, because I've had it my whole life . . . and it wasn't till the family crisis that I wrote *Is life worth living?* on the bills in my wallet.

It's clear my parents were different when I was born—they'd never name me after a Roman poet now. Actually it's a pretty cool name. Ovid was the guy who retold the myths a couple thousand years ago. Like King Midas and his gold fetish; the kid Icarus, who flew too close to the sun; Myrrha, who was turned into a tree.

Mr. Kranks, my humanities teacher, got a real kick out of my name. After the second class, he handed me the Roman Ovid's *Metamorphoses*, a small book in small type, along with a play with the same name.

"Ovid, these are from my personal library. I dug them out last night, just for you." He put his hand on my shoulder. "You should read them."

"OK," I said.

"This one's got all the myths by your namesake, and this modern play is based on it. You'll appreciate them. Let me know what you think."

"O-kay. Thanks."

Jesus, at first I thought maybe Mr. Kranks was coming on to me. But it turned out I read that play three times. I could totally relate in this weird way.

The way I started to see it was that all of us at Lambert High are wrestling with the messes the gods got us into, or we got ourselves into, or our fate designed for us.

Whatever. It seems like we're morphing into creatures of all kinds. Just like in the myths. And we all have our stories—myths, reality, a little bit of both—that somebody knows or everybody knows . . . or nobody knows.

perfect pitch

The minute me, my friend Jack, and his girlfriend walked into the Abyss, this underage club, last Saturday, I knew I was in one of my envious moods. Through the dark of the room, I could see Orpheus (that's what I call him now—lyre, saxophone, what's the difference?) warming up with his band, his jet-black hair under the spotlight. He came over, all smiles, and led us to a table near the front.

After Orpheus hopped back onstage, Jack laughed. "He's got perfect pitch. Someone farted in math the other day, and he yells out 'B flat!'"

When the gig started, Orpheus was so damn smooth on the tenor sax, I could see all the girls at the nearby tables leaning forward. By the time he got to his killer rendition of "Soul Eyes," he really had 'em going.

I mean, Jesus, Orpheus got a girlfriend in record time, right after he moved here to northern California from Chicago last spring. Dalia, no less—"Miss Independent." I wish he'd bottle what he's got with girls—I'd buy a couple cases. Course, so much of it's tied up with his music. It seems like he connects with the girls through his eyes when he's playing.

But he's not a *player.* He's really into Dalia. I wouldn't be surprised to see him serenading her under a window.

And he'd go to Hell and back for her. All the way. No question.

I didn't see him again until today, outside English class. I was scribbling my algebra/trig homework at morning break. He slouched down near me on the low cement wall and stared into space.

"What's up?" he asked.

"Nothin' really. You?"

"Not much," he said. "The band's got another gig at the Abyss in a couple weeks."

"Cool," I said, stuffing my algebra into my notebook.

Orpheus smiled. But the bags under his eyes gave him away. He looked like shit. I'd heard some talk about him and Dalia over the past couple days. Maybe it was true.

Orpheus scratched at the scruff on his chin. For a second, he seemed like he wanted to say something, but he must have changed his mind.

"Catch ya later, Ovid," he said, standing up and shaking out his long legs.

ORPHEUS AND DALIA

Doesn't the rain need the clouds?
Doesn't the ocean need the sand?
Doesn't the wind need the sky?

That's how Orpheus needed Dalia.
And Dalia liked it fine
until she stopped liking it.

"I love you, Orpheus,
like the lightning loves the thunder,
like the mountain loves its trees,
but it'll never work between us
if you don't give me some fucking space.

Give me some space
and we'll be great again.
Just prove you can do it.
Just for a few weeks."

Orpheus didn't call her
didn't text her
didn't email her
didn't find her between classes

until he felt like
rain without a cloud
sand without an ocean
wind with no sky to blow around in

and he sent her a text
just once
just that once:
miss u

And it was over.

venus, are you out there ?

So if I'm going to be perfectly honest, the only guy I know who has his head on straight about girls, about life, is my friend Jack. He's been on top of things since we were best pals in kindergarten, when he got us both into the "Reptile Group" so we could joke and fool around together all day. Now he's got everything mapped out to go to a state school.

His mantra: "Shoot for pretty good grades—a 2.8 GPA—but don't kill yourself. Leave time for varsity baseball and plenty of time for a girlfriend."

Damn. If I had Jack's sense, or anything close to it, I'd open my mouth and do something about this beautiful, spunky girl at Lambert with mocha skin. This girl who will go unnamed. But I can't seem to follow Jack's advice: "Show confidence, Ovid. Just act like you've got your shit together. Girls like that. You can even be kinda artsy, but you gotta at least pretend like you know what you're doing, bro."

Hell, if I could pull that off, I'd be all squared away. That girl would be my girlfriend and my family shit would fade into the background . . .

13

. . . along with that fucked-up thing I do.

Bottom line, I could really use an intervention from the gods—Venus, to be exact. I don't trust Cupid.

all I know

I do have a handle on a couple things in my life, for sure. I can write. And I can draw.

Even Mr. Z., the art teacher, says good stuff about my artwork. Since he sees that I basically live in the art room, he cuts me a lot of slack in Drawing and Painting. Treats me like I'm in some independent study with him. He's really laid back.

"Just paint whatever you want, Ovid. You can ignore my assignments. You'll be needing a portfolio, so start building one up in my class. Do you understand what I'm saying?"

What a cool guy.

When I showed him my latest painting, I don't think he even looked at me funny, the way most people do.

"That bear looks like he's starving, deranged," he said. "The boy seems to be regurgitating the bear. Am I reading that right?"

I nodded. "Or morphing into it."

"You've got quite an imagination in there," he said, tapping my head lightly. "Very interesting. Nice textures. See where it takes you."

During class, I made a lot of progress. I painted all this terrific stuff that comes from a weird dream I keep having, with all these animals in cages. Once I had the shapes of the figures, I attacked the canvas with wide strokes of white, so the colors underneath peeked through. Made it look pretty dreamlike. Then I repainted the figures emerging from the fog and quickly brushed on white again, to build up the surface. I love it when an old line shows through as just a bumpy scar on the canvas. Sometimes throwing paint around and building up the layers on a canvas can feel almost as good as sex—in my limited opinion.

Painting morph-boy, I felt like I was in another dimension, the energy surging from me to the canvas and back. Like magic, the energy took up all the space inside me, so I couldn't think about home or my sister or girls or anything.

What a relief to turn off my mind. It's always working overtime—lashing out at me, playing mind games. It definitely doesn't have my back. Not with the things it thinks up to do to me.

still fall quarter

are obsessions the norm?

ALEXIS FLIES

Alexis's mother called it phar-magification,
smokes that light up your head
your heart
your creativity.

The idea was to smoke weed
together and get closer,

to avoid the mother-daughter friction,
so typical and so annoying.

The idea was to smoke weed on Thursday nights
after homework was done.

But Alexis ran with it:
stoned at school, Monday through Friday,
stoned all weekend
flying as close to the sun as she could get.

Alexis gave her mother that "Fuck you" look
in the kitchen in the morning,
at the dinner table in the evening,
and all the times in between.

The soccer coach kicked her off the team
when she didn't show up for practice.

Then her mom got clean in rehab.
For a while, Alexis was scoring her weed
off Thena (my sister).
Alexis's mom tried to rein her daughter in.
Her dad was exhausted from trying to rope her in.

So Alexis put them out of their misery.
She rolled her parents into a joint.
Smoked them on Thursday.

higher than a kite

We were streaming out of Humanities.

"Hey, no-ass, wanna wait with me in the bleachers?" Alexis said. "My mom's picking me up."

We sat down in the middle of the bleachers, her in the sun, me out. She was wearing soccer shorts and a John Lennon T-shirt that I would have stolen off her back. I was sweating in my jeans. It's always hotter in fall than summer—not sure what that's all about.

Just sitting there next to her, I could feel the muscles *not* rippling under my shirt. I'm actually kind of average. My biggest muscle is in my left calf. That's what I get for skateboarding all over. (Can't get my license because my dad thinks cars + teenagers = trouble + big bucks. He's an econ prof at Taylor.) My best feature, according to Alexis, when she's coherent, is "my mop of light brown hair, flopped over my face."

But her? She's strong. With an enviable six-pack. She even had a mean curveball back in middle school, when we used to get together with Jack, my other friend Duwayne, and some random guys to play baseball on my dead-end street. Alexis beaned Duwayne so hard with one of her pitches, he was out for a couple minutes. She has a mouth, too. We all still quote her, the time she got pissed at Jack: "You're gonna get carpal tunnel from beating off to Victoria's Secret ads. Better alternate hands, *Jack.*"

Alexis bumped my leg as she was lying back to sunbathe. Popped me back into the present.

"I don't care if my mother never comes to pick me up," she said. "I could sit here in the sun with you and fry myself forever. Got any munchies, art-boy?" She looked over at me with bloodshot eyes.

"Want some warm carrot sticks?"

"That all you've got? Nothing with refined sugar . . . or chocolate-covered at least? Carrot sticks sound a little limp . . . like you." She cracked herself up with that comment. But she didn't smile at me, like she used to after some zinger.

I reached for my backpack, ready to leave.

I miss the old Alexis. The one who could razz me without making me feel like shit. I'm hoping it's crouched inside her somewhere, waiting to come out.

I honestly hope she doesn't crash and burn like some female Icarus, flying with oversize wings. She's up way too high already, if you ask me. Ready for a meltdown.

When I stood up to go, Alexis rolled her eyes. "Where ya goin'? I was just kidding, scrawny-ass."

As I skated across the parking lot, her spray-tanned mom drove up in her VW, fluffed up her long wavy hair in the rearview mirror, and adjusted her straw hat. Trying to look like a cool, still-kinda-hippie mom but falling apart inside. It was like she was right out of this dream I keep having.

I watched Alexis silently slide into the backseat. She looked out at me as they drove by.

recurring dream

I keep having this dream of a row of cages filled with animals, tame-enough-looking animals, like sheep and pigs and rabbits. Then I tap the sheep cage, and the sheep's skin falls off, and there's a bear underneath. Or I tap the pig cage and there's a gorilla under the pig. Or sometimes it's the opposite, and a cougar is really a giraffe.

People are so unpredictable, so scary, so layered, I almost can't take it. Like my sister. One night, watching *Clerks* with me for the fifty-ninth time, or reciting Will Ferrell lines, making me laugh till my sides ached and my throat actually went into spasms. The next night, stumbling into my room:

"Wagup, Ovid."

Her breath in my face smelled like stale alcohol— fruity.

"Whadayawant, Thena?"

"I really needatalk . . ."

"It's three-thirteen a.m. Can't it wait? I'm still inside a dream."

"Nooo. Wet dream can wait. I needyanow."

"OK, what's so important?" I sat up slowly and scooted to the edge of the bed.

"Listen, Ovid, I'm not shittin' you. . . ."

"Thena, you better get to bed. You look bad, really bad."

"The truthis, bro, my friends're fucked. The parents suck . . . and you, even you suck. . . ."

"Just go to bed."

"Shit, Ovid. I'm sofuckedup. This is the laz time I'm gettin' wasted. Ever."

Then she puked on my floor. A few flecks hit my bare foot.

Why I love her so much, I don't know.

godlike

When I get around Lambert High's beautiful people, it's all over for me. Nathaniel being one of them. I could see him walking down the path next to the quad today as I finished up my sketch of Mr. Kranks—half toad, half fish.

Nathaniel didn't even notice everyone checking him out as he passed. He loped along uneasily like a skittish cheetah trying to get his bearings outside of the jungle. His tawny-blond curls framing his face and cheekbones, his classic Greek nose lightly tanned, his turquoise eyes as bright as tinted contacts, the lines under his eyes making him look like he was listening to a very sad song 24/7.

He pulled his shirtsleeves down, one after the other, like a twitch.

"Hey, Nathaniel," some girl yelled. "Wait up."

Nathaniel blushed. "Hey."

My mistake was glancing up at this guy the girls call "our resident god." After that, it was like I was watching myself make every move from outside my body. With a checklist going on in my head: *awkward, gangly, crooked nose, chin pimple.*

I brushed some sticky oak leaves off my notebook to derail my thoughts.

I already knew about his mother—how Nathaniel and his dad had moved to a crappy apartment after she left. Everybody knew. One day, I saw him walking down along the creekbed. He didn't see me above him on the bridge. I still remember the sound of him crying.

Nathaniel had no idea I was thinking back to that day as he passed by me and my sketchpad on the grass. But I wanted to shake him. "You've got to stop. Seriously. Trust me, Nathaniel."

But I didn't.

I barely know him.

And besides, it's hard to admit I understand him— between losing somebody and doing that fucking thing I do. I wish like hell I didn't get him at all.

Jesus, I wish like hell there was someone I could talk to . . . who wouldn't think I was nuts.

NATHANIEL

He was the most beautiful boy in the school.
Everyone wanted him, girls and boys.
Even people who had paired off
wanted him just for a night.
Even Orpheus had dreams about him sometimes,
when he wasn't dreaming about Dalia.

Nathaniel would do almost anything for anybody,
except get close,
except for Franny.
He would hang out with Franny
because it seemed like she didn't want him.
She never pushed him either.
She just sat next to him smoking, keeping her distance.
Just listened and echoed back his feelings to him.

The rumors were true,
that Nathaniel's beautiful mother left one day
and never said good-bye.
We'd all heard it in eighth grade.
He'd been searching for his mother on the Internet
ever since,
his dad too broken to pay attention.

But Nathaniel's memories of her were disappearing fast,
like a virus eating text.

So Nathaniel turned into a sculptor,
carving on himself
till streamlets of blood
decorated his arms and legs,
till his skin was as scaly and scarred
as an alligator's back.
His friend Franny understood—
her latest film was *Violence as Beauty*—
but she worried he would carve too deep,
die young like the mythical Narcissus.

But nothing deterred him.
Even in spring, with classrooms
hot as saunas,
Nathaniel never wore shorts or short sleeves.

Everyone wanted to fix him
so they could have him and nurture him,
but his sculpture came first,
always.

cupid's sense of humor

"For our third class, I want you to feel the volume of the figure as you're sculpting. Find the figure inside the clay and let it come out." The sculpture teacher circled the room of mostly adults and me.

My school art teacher, Mr. Z., had recommended the class: "A friend of mine teaches sculpture on Tuesday nights. It'll get you ready for independent study with me next year."

I looked up, and this male model in his twenties walked in and started taking off his robe.

Damn, I thought. I totally liked having female models better. Couldn't stop staring at the pretty model with the long ponytail in the first class. I'd never been allowed to stare at a naked woman for two hours straight in a bright light before. I'd seen my sister by mistake. I'd seen parts of girls, but never the whole thing—besides in movies. Somehow, that first class, I'd made myself look down and dig my hands into the clay.

Working in three dimensions was sweet. Even when there were guy models, like the one last night, who kept breaking his pose to stretch out his knee. Couldn't blame him really.

Strangely, my parents didn't even freak when I signed up for the sculpture class. The details slipped under Mom's radar because of the location: I heard her muttering to Dad as she signed the form, "What trouble could he get into at the Community Center, Marv?"

Good thing they didn't know what went on last night. At break, this woman with loopy earrings, my mom's age, came over and whispered in my ear, "Do you have an extra sculpting tool?" I didn't. But she kept peeking over at me . . . and so did the model.

"Nice, Ovid," the teacher said, looking over my figure. "It would be fun to keep the body rough the way you have it, and make the facial features more detailed for a nice contrast."

But when two hours were up, I wasn't quite done with my head-to-mid-thigh torso of the guy.

"Do you need me to stay a little longer . . . after class?" the guy model asked.

"That's OK," I said, packing up.

The way I figure it, the come-ons in class had Cupid's signature all over them. Cupid was messing with me—by sending me a man and an older woman—'cause he probably got word I was interested in this girl at Lambert.

winter quarter

why do parents
get to screw up?

out of balance

I was having one of those mornings at school where I might as well have hung a CLOSED sign on my brain. Where I'd have been better off just sitting on the semidry bench where I was and staring into space. The words in my physics book jumped around on the page when I tried to concentrate—and I wasn't even on anything (hadn't been for what seemed like forever). There was this quiz coming up on Newton, third period. Something about unbalanced forces, but the only thing I could relate to was "unbalanced."

When I looked up, Dalia waved at me, then spotted Orpheus and ducked around the corner of the building. She is seriously over him. Poor guy.

"Focus," I told myself.

But a girl was coming my way. Her turned-up nose peeked out from under a pink hoodie. Myrra. I was indebted to Myrra. We'd kissed inside a tunnel at the park when we were seven, or maybe eight.

When I think about it, that was the peak of my romantic life. My love life has gone downhill from there.

We hadn't stayed in touch much since elementary school, when I used to love watching her bop around with her friends. Well, actually, she'd helped me once in Chemistry, so she probably understood this Newton stuff. I thought about asking her for help again.

The rain let up for a minute, and Myrra pushed back her hood. Her shiny chestnut-blond hair was wrapped into one of those cute, messy ponytails. As she got closer, the thing I noticed was . . . the sparkle was gone from her eyes.

She seemed not to see me, was concentrating on picking at the peach nail polish on her thumb. But then she glanced at me, and her gray eyes were vacant as fog. She nodded, bit her lower lip, and took off.

Shit. It *was* her—I overheard my mom talking on her phone a couple weeks ago. "You got her some help? She's in therapy? . . ."

I was pretty sure now that the *she* was Myrra. Who else would it be—my mom and her mother talked almost every day.

I connected the dots with another half-heard conversation. Something about Myrra's dad: "He's gone? . . . So glad you came to your senses," my mom said, her phone pressed tight against her ear.

I hadn't seen Myrra's dad up close in years. Our families did holidays together when we were little. The video I had of him in my head was at the Fourth of July picnic in the park, the summer before second grade. Myrra's mom was going on about something: "Yakkity-yack, blah, blah, blah. What did you think, honey?"

"Uh," her dad said in his usual monosyllabic way.

Myrra hugged her dad's leg and begged him to play with her. So he lined up all the kids and tossed a rubber ball to us. He threw mine extra high—maybe to mess me up—but I was all over it every time.

Myrra wiggled and pranced on her tiptoes when it was her turn. Her dad was as charmed by her as I was, even though she always missed.

MYRRA AND HER FATHER

Myrra couldn't quite believe how pretty
she looked in her strappy gown
and high heels,
hair pulled back loosely
to show off new chandelier earrings.

She wanted her father to hug her tight.
She wanted him to say,
"You're my princess,
sweet as a bouquet,
graceful as a dove."

He stared at her,
called her "lovely."
She wanted more than that.

But she didn't want *that*.

The second time he came to her room,
touched her at night,
she felt her girl-soul leaving her body.

She watched as her limbs turned hard and crusty.
Her arms sprouted branches.
Her fingers grew into veined leaflets.

All that was left of her
was a jagged myrrh tree,
its branches intertwined,
inextricably ingrown.

How could she prune and trim
herself down to the girl
hidden somewhere inside?
Ever.

moody frogs

From the window of my room, I can see this gnarly old oak with no leaves. If I think of the branches as picture frames, I can look through and see what's in the picture.

It's like that time we found an empty window frame in the trash by the lake. We held it up and framed stuff with it—very Zen, or whatever. The pebbles on the footpath, my old running shoes with the leather peeling off, the lifted leg of a dog peeing on a bush. And the frogs. But the frogs wouldn't stay in the boundaries of the frame, so we abandoned it and just tried to catch the frogs. They seemed so happy and wild.

We spent hours capturing frogs and letting them go. Me and Thena. We did all that stuff. Mom and Dad encouraged us to be free spirits then. They called Thena "a handful" but were totally into her music, even into her attitude, since she started turning into a teenager.

But it's so weird. When the weather was still warm, a couple months ago, I went back to the park, alone, to the same spot. I caught a medium-size frog, and dammit if he didn't look at me mournfully.

So, bottom line, are the frogs happy or are they depressed?

Or do I just think everyone's in the same mood as me?

THENA AND ME

Me and Thena:
Building blanket forts she turned into séances.
Playing video games instead of doing homework.
Jumping off the roof onto mattresses
when Mom and Dad were out.
Howling at the moon.
Wading in the "possible chem dump/don't-ever-wade-in-
that-creek" creek.
I followed her into battle as if she were Athena.
Whatever she did.
I didn't care about getting in trouble.

And Thena was always strumming her guitar,
the strings squeaking in this melancholy way—
even tried to teach me.
But then she was practicing all the time,
bought herself a used Fender Strat,
joined a band—alternative rock.

Then she started skipping classes,
when she was supposed to be applying to college.
Then she started coming home reeking of alcohol.
Then she wasn't talking to me much,
even when she'd stumble into my room
by mistake and pass out.

Then she did meth
and threw a lamp at Dad
and the parents put her in rehab.
She got sober.
Made me laugh again.
Even took me to a concert—
I was back on her buddy list.

Then she slipped.
Went back to rehab.
Slipped again.
The spastic but predictable dance
got way too familiar.

Thena was center stage
in her own tragedy
of mythical proportions
and I didn't have much of a part to play.
I was mostly backstage, wishing, wanting
to go back to Act I.
Missing her.

Then she left home
and she wasn't coming back.
Even to see me.

from bad to much worse

It's been nine months now with just the three of us at home. Thena gone—maybe living in her beat-up car somewhere. Or maybe out there homeless, roaming the woods like that girl Callisto, who was turned into a bear. Belonging nowhere.

But my sister isn't out on the prowl because Juno's jealous of her. My sister's out there because she's freakin' hooked on meth. And she isn't going to wind up as a constellation in the sky—the ending of her story probably isn't going to be so pretty. It makes me hurt inside to think about it. But there isn't a damn thing I can do for her.

I mean, my parents tried a detective and that led nowhere.

Back when she left, I got up my nerve and talked to a few of her old friends at school. With my best buddy, Jack, standing by me.

"No clue."

"Give it up, man."

"She's gone without a trace. Sorry, dude."

Then, somehow it got worse when it seemed like it couldn't—I turned into my parents' project. They wanted me to be their kid who had nice friends, nice grades, and a nice life. Who they could be proud of. I would go to a nice liberal arts college. Near home. No rocking the boat, which had been badly capsized and had barely been bailed and righted again.

"Addiction runs in families," Mom said. "Your grandmother, your great-grandfather. Your sister."

So they started watching over my every move with amazing intensity. I wouldn't drink or do meth or go to rehab or slip or go back to rehab or talk back or deviate or defy or disobey or disagree or challenge or confront or do anything out of the ordinary that might scare them. I definitely couldn't be myself, with all my twisted thoughts, disturbing obsessions, unsettling anxieties that might unhinge them and mess up the future they've carefully planned for me.

So I've gotten as mute as a moth. Except in my writing and my drawing, which I now keep hidden in my notebook under my mattress, or in my backpack when I leave the house. Because a platypus doing yoga, a kid in a horse halter, wild elephants trapped in nets, just wouldn't go over well.

And then there's the belt—the one I keep on the floor of my closet. What would they think about that?

ulterior motives

"Hey, Ovid," Mei yelled from across the quad.

Mei!

When she got up close, she said, "If you help me load some boxes into my car, I'll buy you lunch. How's that sound? There's plenty of time before fifth period. Put away that soggy sandwich."

Hey, I wondered, *is Venus tuned into my life after all?*

"Sure," I said, pushing my tuna sandwich back into the brown paper bag. I hadn't talked to Mei much since her now-famous "shopping spree." Not like we ever said more than five words to each other. Well, maybe we'd said six words when we were both looking for different books in the library once and ended up practically on top of each other. 823 and 823.8. Isn't it weird how the only two people tracking down books in the library seem to end up in the same space?

Anyway, I followed Mei to the student center, where she had a couple heavy boxes of flyers for the LGBTQ Alliance. I tried not to stare at her.

"There's a march this Friday," she said, touching my palm as she handed me a flyer.

I picked up the box she pointed to and followed her to her Mazda Miata, trying to act more buff than I am. I'm

sure Mei's at least partly into guys, and I don't care about the rumors. I don't care if she's bi, and I don't care if she's an activist just to piss off her mom. She's defiant, feisty, sure, independent, determined, rebellious—everything I'd like to be.

"Oh, damn," she said when she opened her trunk.

It was so crammed with posters and boxes, she had to rearrange everything to fit the new stuff in. While she was shuffling things around, I pictured her in yoga club, in her tights and purple top. I couldn't help it. She drops in sometimes to mellow out. Does this scorpion pose where she's balanced on her mocha-colored forearms, with her legs flipped way back over her head— her body looks like a question mark. She's always helping beginners, like Nathaniel the resident god, who showed up one time and, amazingly enough, had no balance.

After she finally crunched down the trunk, we walked side by side to the deli. Her hair looked as black and shiny as ink spilled on drawing paper—I wanted to touch it so bad. Her green flip-flops thumped on the cold cement. Her jean jacket was unbuttoned. A knit hat was her only acknowledgment that it was 38 degrees.

"You don't have to pay me back," I said. "I'll help you anytime." *Uh-oh*, I thought. *Did I come on too strong?*

"No, I want to buy, Ovid. You're a real sweetie. Get whatever you want."

Do relationships ever start like this? I wondered as I bit into my cheese-and-jalapeño sandwich. My mind kept bringing this up while I was trying to hear what Mei was saying.

"You should come to the march. . . . only thing I care about . . ."

"Sounds interesting," I said, even though I knew I wouldn't be there.

"Nathaniel says I should see your art . . . awesome . . ."

Mei does debate team, so her eye contact is overwhelming. But it wasn't really too much of a hardship to stare into her eyes—two black moons, bewitching and intense. I really like strong girls. God knows why.

QUEEN MIDAS'S TOUCH

She was queen of the hill
almost top of the heap,
climbing up to CEO of her company,
rich as a queen.
Mei's mother.

Mom bought Mei
electronic toys Mei didn't unpack,
designer clothes Mei didn't wear,
a convertible to drive to school.

Mom took phone calls from work
in the middle of school plays
in the middle of debates
in the middle of dinner.

Mom took the call from the police
the day Mei shoplifted:
a $99 belly-button ring
a $79 pair of skinny jeans
a $25 push-up bra
and a $350 fleece jacket—
just enough to make it a felony.

"Why in the world did you need to do that?"
her mom asked.

"You're Queen Midas.
You tell me," Mei said.
"I'm just joining you on your throne
to materiality.
That's your goddess, right?"

Besides, it got you to show up for me.
Didn't it?

over the top

"It's very important that we eat together as a family. It's the most important thing." Mom decided this a few months ago. All part of her shift away from an unflinching focus on Thena leaving—like she suddenly took a look around at who was left in the family.

Now she's been coming home from work exactly on time every day so we can all eat a nutritious dinner together. It was so much better back when she was totally fixated on her work at the state senator's office.

With the "new program," Dad's got a quota of two beers a night.

And my life's been under a high-powered microscope 24/7.

Why I ever showed Mom the College Prep Calendar, with monthly reminders of what to do for college applications, I'll never know. December's pressure-point-of-the-month is PSAT results, and she's constantly checking to see if they've arrived, even though they don't even count.

Literally, nothing in my life goes without comment or scrutiny.

"Most kids I see over at the school have short hair now. You'd look so much cuter if your hair wasn't hanging over your ears like that, Ovid."

She's dreaming if she thinks I'm going to buy into the preppy look.

And last night, it was like a nightmare at dinnertime. All three of us around the table, with no one but me to focus on.

"Obviously, we didn't give your sister enough guidance at a crucial time in her life. We're not letting that happen to you, Ovid," Mom said.

"We didn't pay enough attention," Dad echoed.

"We're parents first," Mom said.

"We're here for you," Dad said.

"Especially in the college process. If necessary, I'll go part-time at my job to help you," Mom said.

I almost choked on my salad.

Stay at your job! I yelled inside.

"Are you listening, Ovid?" Mom asked.

"Yeah," I muttered. *What did I do to deserve this? Dammit, Thena, look what you've done now. Fuck you, wherever you are.*

clay fantasies

The model threw an Indian-patterned sheet on the stuffed chair and sprawled out on it, her leg on the chair arm.

I started with a lump of mocha clay and kneaded it until it was supple under my fingers. I worked out the figure's long thighs and smoothed them with my thumb. Then came her waist, her breasts, her arms behind her head.

When I got to her head, I worked with a pencil to make each strand of long, straight hair. For the face, I used a small tool to make slightly different features from the model's. All my senses were on alert. The touch of the clay warming in my hands. The murmur of the heater. The dryness in my throat.

When I stepped back and looked at the figure, I could see that I'd sculpted the details of Mei's face. It was beautiful. But yikes! Was I going over some line? It was like I was touching her without permission.

I fumbled for my bottled water in my backpack, leaving clay stains all over it.

Then I reworked the eyes and nose to make my sculpture look just like the model.

allthumbs

My phone vibrated in Living Skills. A text from Sophie:
wassup?

I was glad to be distracted from the lecture on sub-
stance abuse. I wish I trusted Sophie as much as she trusts
me. Maybe I could tell her some of what's going on. Hell,
her older sister knew Thena. When Thena disappeared, I
could tell that Sophie knew, just from the gentle look she
gave me. We've been in a couple classes since then—and
my phone's constantly vibrating with her texts. At least
it keeps both of us from dozing off and drooling on our
desks.

But Sophie'll probably get honorable mention in the
senior yearbook for "Biggest gossip." So I hold off telling
her too much.

"Marijuana leads to other hallucinogens. . . ." Mrs.
Hunt was saying.

I texted Sophie back: **nuthin much. wassup with u?**

Besides being totally text-possessed, Sophie's always
on Facebook or MySpace. I mean, almost any hour out of
the twenty-four.

"Just because I fall asleep with my laptop on my stom-
ach doesn't mean anything." She laughed when I told her
to get a life. "Cats love electronics. Did you ever notice

that? My cat, Snorz, sleeps behind the computer and on top of the DVD player. No one gets on his case for that."

I laughed. "Not like you're defensive or anything. . . ."

"Nooo, not me." She slapped me on the arm. "Besides, I've got my surveys to keep up on my blog. People expect it."

And she's gotta spend time on her covert obsession—surfing chat rooms, invisible. That's Soph for you.

Ecstasy, or methylenedioxymethamphetamine, appears to cause . . . Mrs. Hunt was writing on the board.

Another text from Sophie:

u gotta take my new survey. weird habits, quirks, phobias. perfect 4 u

i gotta pass soph (I've got too freakin' much to hide.)

u seen orpheus? he still seems depressed bout dalia

ya

that really sux. hey u mind doin me a favor?

what?

u know any1 4 me? i prefer nerds. online only

It totally wasn't my thing, but I did know someone she might like. This guy Caleb (*robogeek01*) from the high school across town. He was helping my friend Duwayne with the animation for Franny's student film *Violence as Beauty.*

lucky 4 u i know some1 u might like

orly?

ill txt him later

thx ovid

Before I texted Caleb that night, I took a quick look at Sophie's survey:

what do you do that's cute?

what do you still do that you used to do as a kid?

when did your last phobia get to you?

when was your last panic attack? over what?

what do you do that's weird?

what do you do that makes you squirm?

what compulsions drive you?

come on! this is your chance to unload.

I quickly clicked out of it. Damn. It was easier to think about Caleb playing Cupid to Sophie's Psyche — those two lovers who only hooked up in the dark. Cupid had a thing about being anonymous.

Actually, it's perfect. Caleb and Sophie can roll around in the shadows of cyberspace, as faceless as they want to be.

Or whatever. Maybe they won't even like each other.

painting and drawing

"Ink in those last pages. They're ready," Mr. Z. said to my old-time buddy Duwayne. He lets Duwayne work on his graphic novel in class.

"And you, Ovid. Let's take a little time and see what you've been up to. Just for a few minutes. Then you can get back to work. What do you think?"

Mr. Z. stared at my latest canvas. A mucousy-looking creature was emerging from this temple-like building.

"I've got these acrylics . . . and the drawings in my notebook," I said.

He pushed his glasses onto the bridge of his nose and squinted. "OK, I think you need to mix your paints more, on the palette, to keep the colors from looking clichéd. Otherwise, your brushstrokes are fresh. I like the layering. Let's see what you have in there." He pointed at my notebook.

Thank goodness I keep the drawings at the back of my notebook, upside down. That way, Mr. Z. couldn't read me like a tabloid.

"Well, look at these drawings," he said. "Your colors are more subtle here." He ran his fingers through his semigreasy dark hair.

After dragging over a metal chair, he sat down and went slowly from page to page. His short nails were filled with dried paint. His pants were flecked with colors.

When he got to my drawing of Nathaniel, he stopped for a while. Of course, he didn't know the boy swimming with alligators was Nathaniel, resident god.

Mr. Z. spent some time studying my Queen Midas picture of Mei's mom. Then he turned to Myrra, a small person hiding inside a large body.

"I like the symbolism here, Ovid."

"Thanks."

"These would all be stronger if they had a theme."

"Uh . . . they do have a theme."

"Then it needs to be more obvious," he said, patting me on the back. "This is good work. Very intense. You might want to include some more traditional drawings in your portfolio, along with these, to show your technical skill. . . ."

"I don't have anything like that."

"Well, you need to work on some. . . . I must say, I'm amazed at what goes on in your head, Ovid."

Uh, yeah, I thought. *Me, too.*

disconnects

"So what's with the dreds?" I asked my pal Duwayne as we tromped up the stairs to my room to finish our U.S. History project.

His hair, in combination with his green polo shirt and clean white running shoes, made me laugh.

"Just touchin' base with my roots. I'm half black, or didn't you notice?"

My old-time buddy Duwayne and I have been doing projects together since middle school—eases the pain since we're both into writing and drawing.

"So what did ya think of *Running Out*?" he asked, pulling some markers out of his pocket. "Am I the next-Great-American-Graphic-Novelist-in-the-making or what?"

"You just gave it to me two days ago, asshole. I only looked at the pictures."

"How 'bout Paula?" he asked. "She say anything about it? She gives better feedback anyway. She gives better everything actually."

"Shut up, Duwayne, if you ever want me to get to it."

Paula is a goddess in the brains department. Duwayne and Paula and I sometimes look at each other's writing. Paula writes poetry, like me, but much more sophisticated stuff—she's being considered for some anthology.

Duwayne gingerly pulled something covered in plastic out of his backpack. "A sweet first-edition *Spider-Man*. Some sun damage, but not bad, huh?"

"Jesus, how'd you get that?"

"My dad got it on eBay. He must be feelin' guilty about the big dee-vorce."

"Damn."

"Check this out, Ovid." Duwayne rolled up his sleeve and flexed to show off his latest tattoo. Wolverine. Everyone at school keeps track of his fake tattoos. A new one every week.

"You know when your arm was blank, a few weeks back?" I said. "Me and Jack thought you were going off the deep end."

Duwayne nodded. "Yeah. Me, too, man."

I laid out the sheets of poster board I'd gotten for our World War II time line.

"Ya know," Duwayne said, "I fantasized about wreaking havoc on my parents—doing an Iceman and freezing them at status quo. Or freaking them out by setting the school on fire."

"OK . . ."

"But all I did was that graffiti in the library bathroom. . . ."

"That was you? *Long live Donnie Darko*? That rabbit was cool, but it wasn't your usual style."

"Didn't wanna be recognized, man."

"Right," I said, flattening the poster board with some books.

We mapped out the time line and drew the whole damn thing while we talked. It took all afternoon.

I started thinking I could tell him a little bit about what was going on with me. So as he was packing up, I mumbled, "Hey, Duwayne, you got a minute before you leave?"

But he must not have heard me, because he didn't even look up.

"There's a typo here," he said, leaning over the time line. "Two *n*'s in *Poland*. Can you fix it? I gotta go help my mom with some yard work."

Jesus, I felt like I was stuck with my own damn mythology—that fucked-up thing I fucking do—and nowhere to unload it.

I watched his scrawny ass ducking out the door, and I wasn't about to pull him back, even though I wanted to.

Oh well, he's got enough of his own shit to worry about.

Duwayne and the Divorce Shuttle

Like Proserpina shuttling
between earth goddess, Ceres,
and underworld king, Pluto,
Duwayne flitted back and forth
between his parents.

His mother dear said,
"Summer, summer, summer."
His father dear said,
"Winter, winter, winter."

He tried to take refuge in spring
to keep himself from splitting in half.

But
like a magician's assistant,
like the shells of a cracked crab,
like a two-headed creature,
like Proserpina living in the light and the dark,

Duwayne was split in half,

until he found his own season—fall.

While he watched his parents
freezing over,
heating up,
following their own internal thermostats,

Duwayne changed his colors
according to his own clock.

hair balls

I wish like hell my parents would stop ganging up on me, two on one. Course, they think they're doing the right thing—they both have the same agenda for me: a normal, healthy life. Which lately translates into them checking online for my test grades, calculating and recalculating my grade-point average, inspecting my pupils, searching my room covertly for drug paraphernalia (that's what I'm guessing because the thread is sometimes missing from my bedroom door), trying to hack into my email (one time they left up *invalid password*), interrogating ("Who's that kid with the pierced lip you were talking to when I picked you up for the dentist?"), and ordering college brochures from preppy places with sunny-faced students on the covers who would never think of doing anything but studying.

And then there's the mantra of the week.

Last week it was "Decent SAT scores, decent SAT scores, decent SAT scores, ooooom."

I bare my teeth and shout back: "SATs don't matter for art college!"

But nothing comes out. It's all inside. I'm gagging. Like I've got a hair ball with all this unsaid crap tangled up in it. God knows what would happen if I coughed up the hair ball and presented it to them, or if I showed them my sketches. Jesus, if my parents saw my drawings, they'd probably freak out and clamp down on me even more, if that's possible.

I wish I could have known my parents when they were in college. Could have talked to them then. I actually like to hear them tell it and retell it: "Your dad and I met in a classic poetry class. Sappho. Ovid. Homer. Everyone recited something every week, and your father read poetry so beautifully. We named you and Thena to remember where it all started."

Hell, even last year, Mom was taking poetry classes. And Dad would drag out his guitar when he'd had more than a couple beers. But Thena beat every poetic bone out of their bodies. They walled up that part of themselves, and it'd take a lightning bolt to crack them open again.

And then there's me. I'm left like Io in the myths— changed to a heifer so Juno wouldn't vaporize her, guarded by the hundred-eyed monster Argus.

That's me all right.

With my parents standing guard.

And me trying to speak, but wandering wordlessly. Myself hidden inside.

Ready to implode.

scabs

"I've got all these missed calls from out of state," Mom said breathlessly, flipping open her phone.

"Think it's Thena?" Dad asked, moving next to her.

"Don't recognize the number. Do you?"

Dad slipped on his glasses and looked closer. "Go ahead and call it."

Mom dialed.

"Hello," Mom said. "I'm returning someone's call. Have you been trying to reach the Goldings? . . . You're sure? Do you know Thena Golding, by any chance? . . . No? Sorry. Someone must have dialed the wrong number."

It was like picking off a scab. Mom went up to her room to lie down, comatose. Dad grabbed a beer from the fridge and downed it. I couldn't breathe.

Later that night, they reacted by cracking down on me again. As if I didn't want the calls to be Thena, too.

"Curfew's back to ten thirty."

"I'm in high school."

"No discussion."

"Why don't you just plant a freakin' chip in my forearm," I said. Out loud!

Mom just stared at me—it was the first time I'd talked back since Thena left, almost a year ago. Mom didn't even have a comeback.

spring quarter

is everyone *paired off?*

poet extraordinaire

"Duwayne said you got in that love poem anthology. Wow!" I said, walking next to Paula, the brainy poet. We were both carrying our skateboards through the parking lot.

A bunch of girls, passing us, screamed in unison about something or other. Girls get to shriek anytime they want to.

"I haven't really taken it in yet," Paula said, shaking her red-dyed hair into her eyes, hiding her smile.

"Is it that poem, 'Letter to a John'?"

"Yeah!"

" 'I could be some sort of beautiful monster, perfect in my deformity. Could I tell you these dreams? Me as monster, mason, manager of rhymes?' " I said.

"You memorized my poem?" Paula asked, eyes wide.

"Some of it," I said. "It was awesome."

Paula dropped her skateboard and sat on it to tie her red Converse. She'd been skateboarding partway home with me some days. Her matching red hair swung forward, long in front, short in back. With her funky vintage dresses, or whatever you call them, and her thick black glasses, she'd make a great subject for a painting. If

I painted her, I'd make her head transparent, with poems inside. She's got the opposite of writer's block. It's pretty cool.

"So do you think a person can be born devoid of compassion? Huh, Ovid?"

"Seems possible," I said. Her questions were never light. "Is that what you're worried about, Paula?"

"Mmmm." She hoisted her heavy backpack onto her back. She's Harvard-bound, no doubt about it. Or maybe Sarah Lawrence. "I sometimes wonder if competition can coexist with compassion," she said. "I almost didn't lend my notes to somebody who was sick because she's my competitor in Humanities. I hate that about myself."

"But you help Franny with her film all the time. You don't seem competitive with her," I said. "I always see you toting around her tripod, hanging it off the sides of buildings. Looks cool."

Paula turned away.

"Hey, how's the film going, anyway?" I asked. "*Violence as Beauty*—what a title. Duwayne hasn't stopped talking about it since Franny asked him to do the animation."

"I wouldn't know anything about that," Paula said.

So Duwayne was right about Franny and Paula.

I thought he was just making stuff up.

THE CHASE: FRANNY AND PAULA

Franny was munching half a pickle for lunch
and gulping from a half-gallon bottle of water
when Paula first met her.
The body is 2/3 water after all.
Water would fill her up.

Franny was never without her video camera,
making an intriguing film, *Violence as Beauty,*
full of flashy montages
mixed with jazzy slo-mo.

Paula was straight.
She knew it for sure,
or for pretty sure,
but she had a crush on Franny's mind,
on the way Franny led her mind down paths
she'd never explored—
Franny was her muse, her woodland nymph.
She had a crush, too, on Franny's intimate way
of holding a cigarette and talking very close to your face
while at the same time keeping you
at a safe distance with her eyes.

Paula pursued Franny ceaselessly,
like Apollo chasing Daphne
through the thickets,

through the rough underbrush,
oblivious to Daphne's disinterest,
trailing after the huntress relentlessly,
unaware that Cupid's golden arrow had pierced his skin.

And what of the elusive Franny?
She talked about food constantly,
but that was the extent of her intake.
Her head was like a beautiful oversize egg
perched atop a body made of sticks.

Paula imagined that Franny had made a deal
with the Fat Demon somewhere along the way:
that the Fat Demon (or was it Bacchus?)
would leave Franny skinny and bony
if she honored him by constantly gorging
and purging.

Paula spent several lifetimes
trying to understand Franny
trying to help Franny
trying to cajole Franny
trying to get close to Franny
while Franny grew thin as a twig,

until Paula woke up one morning
and she couldn't find her own life
anywhere:

under the covers,
in the closet,
beneath her books,
in her backpack,
on Facebook,
in the mirror.

Paula's life was as tenuous
as a brown leaf
clinging to a stark winter branch.

As much as it hurt to the bone,
made her feel selfish,
made her feel piggish,
made her feel like she wanted to die young,
she dropped Franny cold turkey.

And then she waited.
She waited for her own life
to reappear

like the sun rising
on the horizon
behind Apollo's chariot,
after banks of storm clouds
have cleared away.

drawing and painting critique

Mr. Z. got a good laugh when he saw me putting the finishing touches on my drawing of Franny, Paula's ex-crush. Franny was perched on the bare belly of this obese guy. I wasn't sure if Mr. Z. was laughing with me or at me this time.

"Sure makes me curious about the context of this one, Ovid. Do you have any more you want to share? Ones I haven't seen?"

I turned to the drawing of the girl with her home on her back. At first I was sorry I'd opened to that page. Then I realized that people at school knew about Thena, but that Mr. Z. would never make the connection.

"How do you think these up, Ovid?" he asked.

Then he gave me a strange look. He'd never done that before.

Shit.

visitation from a fallen goddess

I sometimes picture myself showing Thena some of my art stuff and telling her about the parents' recent obsessions. Course, if Thena was here, none of this shit with Mom and Dad would be happening. But I could still picture it—her sitting on my bed, meditation-style.

"The parents don't know, or wanna know, the first thing about me, I'd say to her. They pretend like they can delete the messy, dark parts of me. . . . Wish I could tell you. . . . Never mind. . . ."

"You've got dark parts, kiddo?" she would say, punching my arm.

"They see me as their last hope, 'The Savable Brother of the Designated Addict.'"

"That would be me," Thena'd say.

"The parents are thinking if I make one mistake, I'm doomed."

"So I'm already doomed, huh?"

"Shut up for a minute, Thena. Really, it's ugly. They're on constant alert to save me from anything that looks like a land mine, big or small."

"Sounds like a shitload a fun. . . ."

"You had to be this brilliant musician who royally fucked up. . . . Now they think any kinda artist is headed for the deep end."

"So are you?"

"Yeah! I am going off the deep end, just not in the way they think I am. Already have. Behind my closed door."

"What the fuck are you doing in your room, bro?"

"Listen, you wouldn't even recognize them. They're making me crazy, as crazy as you."

"Thanks for sharing, asshole. So what are you doing in your room?"

"I'd have to guzzle meds to be this straightlaced kid they want, with a cute little painting hobby. Don't they get that I've got to be an artist . . . for the rest of my life?"

"Obviously the fuck not."

"Everything'd fade to this dull gray if I couldn't draw what I need to draw. So what if it's weird shit? I gotta do it to feel like I belong in this virtual unreality of a world."

"I totally getcha, buddy, but you are kinda weird, Ovid." She'd grin and wink.

"Shut up, Thena! Just shut up!"

"Down, boy, down. Chiiill."

I pop out of my head and I'm sitting in my room. Alone.

Bottom line, does it really matter if my parents *get* me?

Somebody did

. . . my sister.

that jock swagger

I should have known something was up when my best buddy, Jack, adjusted his baseball cap and fell into the swagger he normally reserves for his jock friends—chest out, chin up, jaw set, as if to say, "There's nothin' life can throw at me that I can't handle."

Me and Jack and Duwayne were heading toward the far field at lunch to toss around a Frisbee. Suddenly, Jack threw his pack down on the grass and started kicking the shit out of it. Not at all like "Mr. Cool."

"What the hell?" Duwayne said.

"Damn spiders. I hate 'em!" Jack said.

Actually Jack's scared of them—a weak link in his chain.

When the spider was good and dead, Jack pulled out the Frisbee. We spread out and whipped it back and forth. One of Jack's throws was so hard it practically ripped the skin off my hand. He dove for a wild one and flipped over, came up with a green streak on his T-shirt. We hooted and howled.

Sometimes I think girls kind of ruin it for guys—I mean, when we wake up and get interested in them. Jack used to call all the time: "Hey, dude, roll outta bed. We're all meetin' at the park for mud football." Then he hooked up with his girlfriend, Venicia, and we hardly ever saw him anymore—which I can understand and all, considering Venicia. Heck, I'm envious. But most girls have zero tolerance for stuff like farts and burps. Or jokes about tits and ass. Or guys hanging out all afternoon playing football. Course, Alexis was the exception. She was one of the guys before she took up "flying" full-time. Anyway, the fact that Jack had time to toss the Frisbee should have clued me in.

"Hey," Duwayne said, checking his watch. "I gotta connect with Franny. She was all over the animation I did for her film. Can you believe it? She might enter it in some film festival—not just put it up on YouTube. Hey, later."

Once Duwayne was a dot in the distance, Jack threw the Frisbee at his backpack, dropped onto the grass, and proceeded to shoot my illusions about him and Venicia to hell.

JACK AND VENICIA

Jack and Venicia were
attached at the hip,
2 buds on a branch,
2 birds of the same feather,
2 peas in a short pod—
The Couple.

Arms touching in the library
as they hovered over their books,
cropped hair bristling in sync
as they jogged around the track at lunch,
their nudges, their winks,
their piddly fights
were the envy of many,

till Jack went away to baseball camp
and that boy from another school
showed up
with the long curls
and the smile/snarl.
Dangerous.
Forbidden fruit.

Jack heard them,
Venicia and that bad boy.

He heard them long distance:
"Touch it right here,"
he heard her say.

Jack laughed off Venicia's explanations
of a trip to a petting zoo.

She finally admitted
she felt like a dog,
a boar, a bear,
a hairy beast.
She'd only gone down on that other boy.

But Jack never forgave her.

She constantly asked herself,
"How did Jack know? How did Jack hear?"
He constantly asked himself,
"How could she have done it?"

How could Jack have heard
since no one saw,
no one knew?

Simple.
Her phone.

It had jostled in her pocket
and speed-dialed Jack by mistake,
betraying her while she betrayed him.

fuckin' A

I felt so bad for Jack. I'd never seen him hang his head like that. Might have been better if he'd never known about Venicia. Why do girls like bad boys anyway? It's such a cliché. Hell, even Venus was into Mars, and he was supposed to be good-looking and violent. Her blacksmith husband caught them cheating by rigging up this golden spiderweb around the bed—fixed them.

But I didn't mention that to Jack.

Of course, *I* got paranoid. I felt like testing out my phone in my pocket right then and there. What would someone hear if my phone did that? Me swearing into my pillow in my room? My parents discussing colleges at the dinner table? Me doing that thing I do?

That thing I do ... that thing I do ... that thing I do ... that thing I do ... Shit, my mind was stuck on one fucking image.

Jack was chowing down on his turkey sandwich, starting to perk up with some protein. And then it happened.

My mouth opened, and it was like Pandora's box. I started talking and I couldn't stop. Everything came flying out.

"My belt. I whip myself. With my belt. Since fall. I picked up this belt. From the floor of my closet. Started hitting. Started hitting myself with it. Till I was whipping it around. Really hard."

I balled up my fists and tried not to look at Jack. "My parents. My sister. I'm going nuts. It hurts like hell. But the fucking thing stops me from thinking. From feeling anything else."

I looked down at the grass. "And I've been thinking up other things . . . hanging myself . . . not to off myself, just to . . . Jesus, I sound like I'm crazy . . . I'm scaring the shit out of myself."

When I looked up at Jack, he'd stopped in midbite and was looking at me, eyes wide.

Then he was talking: "Shit, dude. Are you all right? That's heavy stuff. If you need anything . . ." He flipped off his baseball cap and ran his fingers through his hair. "Listen, man, maybe you're just going through a rough streak—it happens, dude. You just really gotta stop beatin' yourself up over that shit."

He smiled with one side of his mouth. "Literally."

Then we were laughing. That laugh where we didn't know if we were laughing or crying.

And it seemed like I'd just gained ground in a fucking high-stakes tug-of-war with myself.

adventures in cyberspace

Every time I go to Living Skills, I wish I'd signed up for the online version. You can do that for some classes at Lambert now. Course then I'd miss watching Sophie operate. She sits there, thin blond hair and bangs framing her round face, serious creases between her eyebrows — the conscientious student. But behind a book or under the desk, she's texting faster than anyone else in school.

Lately they've been some version of:

calebs so cool. i owe u ovid

Actually, Caleb's so uncool, such a dork, that he's almost cool. I've known him since this computer-geek camp my mom signed me up for one summer. He was into robotics even back then. "Go ask Caleb," the counselors would say to the kids with the complicated questions.

Instead of the usual this morning, Sophie just texted me **later.** That night she'd practically written one of those Japanese cell phone novels by the time she finished her message.

Sophie and Caleb, aka Psyche and Cupid

For Sophie (sn *allthumbs44*)
when Caleb (sn *robogeek01*)
entered the nerds-only chat room,
it was cyberlove at first site.

He admitted he was a virtual *homo sapien*,
spent all his awake hours tunneling around
the innards of his PC, building tiny robots,
playing video games,
so much that his brother threatened to piss
on his computer.

Sophie admitted it, too.
(Not about the pissing—
about the video games.)

Caleb admitted that his dog, Wasp, was his best friend.
Sophie fessed up to a similar relationship
with her cat, Snorz.

He admitted he was technically a virgin
and that he was in love with sci-fi and fractals.
Her, too (re: the technical virginity).

They played virtual chess every night.
She won 63% of the time.

Then they arranged to meet on Tuesday.
A half hour after school let out.
At the mall.
Her with a red cap.
Him with a blue cap.

She got there early—dizzy, disoriented.
She stared into a store window
filled with bony mannequins.
Then she saw his reflection in the glass,
pulling off his blue cap so fast
he knocked the glasses off his gaunt face.
He'd seen her from behind!
He was obviously into skinny chicks.

She ran home,
back into hiding,
back into the comfort of cyberspace.
Morphed into anonymity, invisibility.

When she bumped into him
in a chat room a week later,
he admitted he'd split that Tuesday
because he knew his real looks, his real self,
would ruin everything.

So they started up where they'd left off,
rebonded online only
and kept it virtual.
It was the best thing
they'd ever had going for them.

virtually yours

Sweet—a happy ending. Finally. For somebody.
Kind of.

Sophie and Caleb are cool. But there's no way *I'm* going to live my life in virtual reality, all in my head.

I've got to talk to *her.* I've got to talk to Mei.

the bomb

I positioned my phone out of sight, next to my thigh, and read the text message. It was in the middle of Mrs. Hunt's lecture on STDs. From Sophie, of course.

i thnk orpheus was checkin mei out at lunch. did u c?

I didn't answer back. I didn't hear another word about HIV, crabs, genital herpes, genital warts, chlamydia, gonorrhea, or syphilis—that last one not to be confused with the poor sucker in the myths, pushing a boulder up a mountain.

Orpheus and Mei? Shit!

I texted Mount Olympus:

venus u gotta help me

still spring quarter

metamorphosis

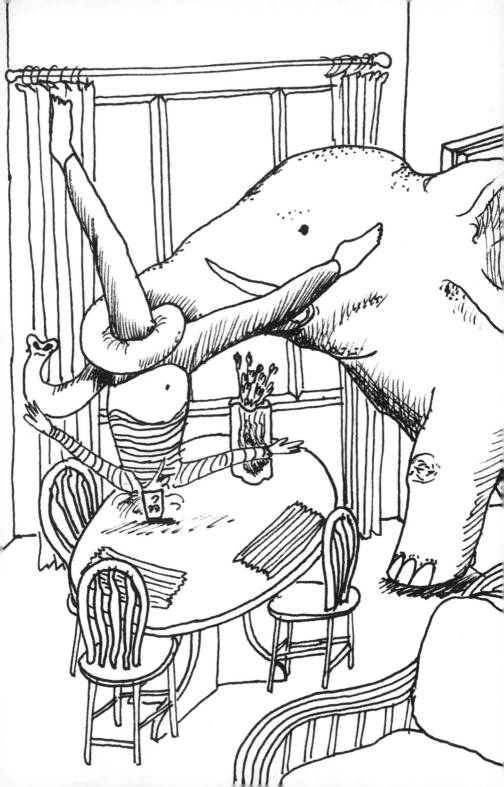

slam dunk

So I was walking through the parking lot with my phone warming up my ear, listening to a message from Jack, when I saw Mei heading toward her convertible. It felt like Venus swatted me on the ass and pushed me, because I actually made myself catch up with Mei. Unbelievable.

"I'd really love to talk, Ovid, but I've got to run or I'm in trouble. I've got community service at the convalescent hospital for the next five months. Bedpans aren't my thing, but that's the way it goes."

Must be for when she shoplifted, I thought. My mouth opened and closed, and then somebody's voice that sounded like mine said, "Wanna hang out on Saturday? Maybe a movie or something?"

She inhaled. I got ready to put on my fake smile. "I'd like to," she said, "but I'd better give you a rain check. I don't have a minute with this bedpan routine, and my mom sort of grounded me."

I smiled. "No problem. See ya later." Then I turned away, pretending I had somewhere to go.

I slumped down under a maple tree. Sat there and inspected my wounds. The way she turned me down was pretty skillful. But I felt sick. The voices started in: *You were stupid to ask her. You're deluded. Made a fucking fool of yourself. You can't be trusted!*

Ohmigod. The crazy shit again.

I might as well have had that belt in my hand. *You're crazy. Weird. Stupid! You goddamned idiot. What were you thinking? Idiot boy. Fucking idiot boy!*

"Shut up!" I yelled. *"SHUT UP!"*

It was quiet.

Something was tickling my arm. An ant was crawling, stumbling over my hairs and making his way down toward my wrist. He walked out onto my pinkie, hung over the edge, and looked like he was about to fall off. When he regained his balance and tottered over to my ring finger, I let him climb off onto the tree. The bark was dark brown and musty-smelling. The leaves were shuffling in the breeze. Some had wormholes, like lace. I could feel the roots of the tree under my legs. I started breathing again. Didn't even know I'd been holding my breath.

Then the crowd cheered from the baseball game across the parking lot.

I thought about Mei again.

I'd actually fucking talked to her, asked her to a movie.

Maybe she really was too busy to go. Yeah, right.

Whatever. I asked her and it didn't work out.

Fuck, I wish she'd said yes.

But what made me think I had a chance?

Hell, I did it. Even if it was a mistake.
I'm a fucking human being—like anybody else.
Gotta fucking give myself a break.

The crowd cheered again. I pictured myself finding Jack after the game. And I pictured me and him laughing about what happened with Mei. Laughing and joking.

What a concept.

The whole thing suddenly didn't seem worth beating myself up over. It just didn't. Not this time, anyway.

aftershocks

"Use specific detail in your stories and try to be emotionally honest." With only two minutes left and counting in Humanities, Mr. Kranks was talking really fast and looking particularly toadlike.

Venicia and I walked out together. Left, right, left, right, in rhythm. She popped out her headphones but avoided my eyes. I thought I heard Sean Lennon. It was cranked up really high.

"I know you heard about me and Jack breaking up," she said. "So are you, like, still talkin' to me?"

"If you're still talkin' to me," I said. She bumped me, shoulder to shoulder, and smiled. Not the smile I was used to, though. Not the smile she'd flash when she was sitting between me and Jack at the movies, holding the big buttered popcorn for all of us. Not even the cute little smile she gave me when I kept asking, "You got any more of them homemade cookies?" at one of Jack's baseball games.

She didn't say anything while we walked toward the library. Then I remembered that Venicia and Mei hung out sometimes — Mei'd probably told her about turning me down. I hoped like heck Venicia wouldn't bring it up.

She ran her fingers through her short hair and it bounced back. Kinda flirty.

"I wish I could get back with him, Ovid. . . . I'd do anything," she said. "Be whatever he wants."

Don't say that, I wanted to tell her. *Just be your freakin' self. Who else're you gonna be?* "It's gotta be hard," I said.

Regrets: Venicia, of Jack-and-Venicia Fame

Venicia wasn't who Jack thought she was.
Wasn't always sunny inside.
Depressed sometimes
when she was alone.

So she molded
herself to fit Jack,
to be the girl he wanted.

Then she betrayed herself and him —
fell off the pedestal,
fell from grace,
fell from goddesshood.

Venicia got a new
phone — a flip phone
that couldn't, wouldn't,
speed-dial by mistake.

She wanted to resculpt herself,
do a Pygmalion —
keep only the sweetness,
blot out the shadowy, cheating parts.

Be perfect again.
So there'd be a chance
Jack would want her back.
A chance of being Jack's
dream girlfriend again.

Heck, maybe no one would want her
like she really was.

home sweet home

I used to think some people were the favorites of the gods, didn't have any defects. But it's just like my dream of poking the sheep and out from under the sheep's skin comes a bear. Everybody's got hidden stuff, even the people who don't look like it.

People like me.

Shit, how long was I going to stay hidden like that miserable heifer-girl, Io, in the myths? How long was I going to stay quiet? Even Io had the balls to write a note in the sand to her father. Philomela wove her damn tapestry to rat on her brother-in-law. Pandora never did shut the lid of that fucking box.

Here I was thinking Venicia should be herself! What about me? Something started building up inside me. By the time I was a block from home, I was a bull, pawing at the ground.

Inside, Dad was reading the paper. Mom looked up from making tacos.

"Hi, Ovid. How was school? I made all the plans for the college visits. I'll show you at dinner. Just you and your dad are going. I thought you'd like that."

I snorted. Darted up the stairs, two at a time. Grabbed my notebook and pulled out the drawings, one after the other. With the papers in my fist, I headed downstairs. All over the living-room floor, I laid my drawings out. My hands were shaking.

Dad craned his neck and came in. Mom marched in with her scarf flowing behind her.

"Look! I'm an artist!" I yelled. "This is what I draw! You go look at the colleges. I'm going to art school!"

They stared at me. Stood there like two scared kids.

Then they stared at the drawings.

"This is me. Take it or leave it." I left Mom and Dad standing there and stomped up the stairs. Slammed the door. Sat on the bed and shook. I heard them downstairs:

"What are we going to do?"

"Nothing," Dad said. "Leave him alone."

With my skateboard under my arm, I slipped out the back door. Rode around for hours. Watched it get dark. Listened to a chatty night bird and the swish of traffic and the clacking of my skateboard on the patched street. My mind was clear for once.

When I got home, I took a couple cold tacos up to my room. Dad had taped a note to the door: *I'm so sorry. Let's talk when you're ready. Give your mother some time.*

At about eleven, I went downstairs and collected my drawings. Taped them to my walls. Put one on my door. On the outside.

I thought I'd never fall asleep. Inside and out, I was vibrating. But I did sleep. And I didn't take the drawings down in the morning. Left them up for anyone to see.

almost summer

closing up shop

no prom scene

School's almost over. In teen movies, things get wrapped up at the end of the year, when everyone goes to prom and totally unexpected couples pair up. Like my buddy Jack would end up with the filmmaker Franny, him in a tux and her in a dress, or vice versa. Sophie would emerge from cyberspace wearing a Cinderella dress and looking more beautiful than anyone—would dance with Caleb, who would suddenly know how to fox-trot. My sister would come back, clean and sober, and help me get ready for the prom. And on and on.

But things aren't like that, as far as I can tell. It seems to me that we all navigate our way through high school— solo or in ever-shifting pairs or groups—trying to find some rhyme or rhythm, some sense.

Sometimes we throw light on our faces, letting other people get a glimpse of us. Then we retreat.

Seems like we're all just groping our way through a labyrinth, fighting our personal minotaurs, morphing into who we really are, like it or not. And along the way, we cross paths with other people.

There's no golden thread to follow. That's for sure. So we all just try to help each other through the maze.

epilogue

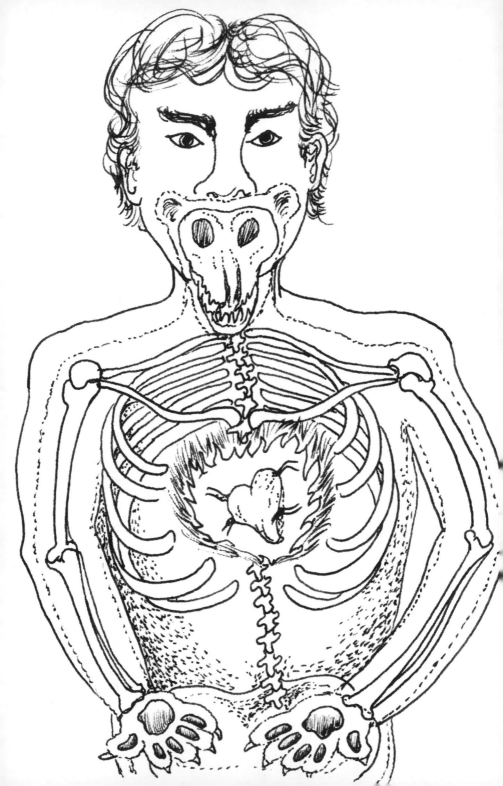

The Roman poet Ovid wrote an epilogue for his book. So I've got one, too (instead of a prom scene—since I didn't actually go to prom).

My pal Jack finally forgave Venicia and they got back together, two peas in a pod. Six weeks later, they agreed to break up. Venicia wasn't who Jack thought she was. Jack wasn't who Venicia thought he was. They still jog together.

Myrra's still in therapy about her dad. She's just starting to be willing to even consider finding her "girl inside" again. Oh yeah, she's been coming to yoga every once in a while.

Mei's CEO mother still prefers her board meetings to spending time with, or understanding, her activist daughter. But Mei's grandma moved in—she's pretty cool, from what Mei says.

Franny encouraged Nathaniel to carve in wood. He carves animal totems that everyone wants, and he's OK with that. He still cuts himself when he's really stressed.

Franny doesn't want to talk about where she is with her food or anything else. Not even her film *Violence as Beauty*, which she says speaks for itself. It'll be shown at the mediaonthedge festival. Duwayne got credit for the opening animation, and he's definitely talking it up.

Orpheus is still playing sax and still isn't over Dalia.

Alexis, the weed queen, has been to a few NA meetings, basically because her mom won't let her get her driver's permit if she doesn't. Alexis keeps her eye out for my sister, Thena, but I'm not holding my breath.

Duwayne's divorced parents hardly ever interact anymore. They're both dating. He negotiates his way between them and is madly at work on his next-great-American graphic novel, *Heroguy*. I read his first one, *Running Out*—it was very cool. Needs a little cutting.

Caleb and Sophie are very tight in cyberspace.

And me? I've been hanging out with Paula. Yeah, the brainy poet Paula, who had the crush on Franny. She likes my drawings. I like her metaphysical questions, and she listens to me. Right now, though, she's pissed that I don't communicate enough.

But I've always got my writing and my art. My latest painting has a bear in a boy's skin . . . or a boy whose insides are lined with a bear.

And I don't even care when people look at it funny.

ACKNOWLEDGMENTS

Thank you to Ovid for writing *Metamorphoses* thousands of years ago. And to Mary Zimmerman for writing *Metamorphoses, A Play*, which was performed not only on Broadway but also at Palo Alto High School, where I saw it. I'm indebted to the actors and to Kristen Lo, who brilliantly directed and staged the Paly High play. I attended three times and would have gone a fourth, but decided I'd better start writing my own take on Ovid's myths.

Along the three-year journey of writing this novel, many people came to my rescue. My oldest son, James Franco, gave a green light to the concept — thought it was intriguing. My youngest son, Dave Franco, read a draft of the book, assured me it was definitely worth working on, and constantly advised me about my characters and contemporary jargon. Both of them supported the book by agreeing to read the audio version.

Rachel and Julie Schuck read an early draft and pressed me to write more about Ovid. Casey Weiss, former editor of the Palo Alto High School newspaper, did a very insightful job of editing the manuscript and insisted that I keep the quirky elements. Susan Hart Lindquist, a fellow writer and mentor, helped me restructure the novel in ways that made all the difference.

My son Tom Franco's illustrations tipped the balance. He let me use drawings from his sketchbooks as inspiration for the paintings and drawings described in Ovid's notebook. Many details about the characters were sparked by those drawings, which, as it turned out, actually ended up as illustrations in the book.

My critique group members, Caroline Goodwin, Shirley Klock, Pam Mayer, Leslie Perkins, JoAnne Wetzel, and Caryn Yacowitz, read the manuscript over and over, giving me wonderful suggestions and making me realize that I couldn't see beyond my nose.

The creative writing students in Jamie Hanmer's classes at Palo Alto High School, particularly Ashley Lamb, and the students in Arantxa Arriada's classes at Los Altos High School critiqued the chapters from a contemporary point of view. While taking a poetry class with David Roderick and Robin Ekiss at Stanford Continuing Ed, I received guidance on the poetry, diction, and syntax in the book. Brian Laidlaw, a poet-musician, gave me important questions to consider about the journal format and about Ovid. Laurie Garcia expanded my knowledge of the Internet, where she says she spends way too much time. And Kelly Hafner helped with texting.

Nick Godin, a high-school student, provided detailed advice about the idiosyncrasies of the characters I'd created. He brainstormed with me for hours and set me straight about high-school culture.

I owe my character Ovid for helping me shine a light on some of the parts of myself I didn't understand, and Maria Damon for helping me sort it all out.

I could never have written the book with confidence without all the people who contributed. And I thank the gods, particularly Calliope, for my editor, Mary Lee Donovan, who always seems to understand my strangest work.

WHO WAS OVID?

In Book One of *Metamorphoses*, the Roman poet Ovid describes the universe on the brink of Creation as "chaos, a raw and undivided mass . . . with warring seeds of ill-joined elements compressed together." More than two thousand years after Ovid's book was published, the "warring seeds of ill-joined elements" are nowhere more obviously center stage than in a modern American high school.

After reading *Metamorphoses*, loaned to him by his humanities teacher, a contemporary high-school junior named Ovid, the main character in Betsy Franco's novel, becomes obsessed with the idea of metamorphosis. By observing his classmates, he can attest to the fact that nothing is ever quite what it seems and that nobody's identity is ever totally certain or static. Like the gods, mortals hide behind masks and take on other shapes and forms in order to deceive, discover, and survive. In short, Ovid and his friends are engaged in a perpetual struggle to make sense of a world that appears unpredictable and absurd—essentially chaotic. At the same time, they are embarking on a journey of defining and transforming themselves.

Not only does high-school junior Ovid share his name with the ancient Roman poet, but intense pressure to conform to his parents' wishes. In Betsy Franco's novel, Ovid's mom and dad want him to stop spending so much time in his room and get involved in "normal" activities, like joining clubs, playing sports, studying for

SATs, and visiting colleges. Ovid would rather be sculpting, painting, drawing, and writing poetry, and he desperately wants to go to art school.

The original Ovid, born in Italy in 43 BC, was sent to Rome as a boy to get an education, a privilege available only to wealthy families. The primary goal of education at that time was to produce fluent and convincing public speakers. Ovid ultimately rebelled and rejected the path that would lead to a safe career as a lawyer or politician. Instead, he pursued his own true love: literature.

Beginning in AD 1, Ovid worked on two books, one of which was *Metamorphoses*, his own take on the Greek and Roman myths. He wanted to give the tales a fresh form, and sometimes combined stories in order to more sharply define the themes that fascinated him: transformation, outward appearance versus true identity, the constant state of flux of the universe, and man's thirst for immortality. His other book was called *The Art of Love*. Both books were written in a surprisingly erotic, fun, and exciting style.

In AD 8, Ovid was sent into exile for reasons that remain somewhat mysterious. Some scholars believe that it was for writing a poem that offended someone in a position of power or that inadvertently spilled some state secret or plot. Some believe it may have been for writing about adultery, which was a crime punishable by banishment. And some believe it was for "error," which most likely refers to his guilt by association in a scandal mixing sex and politics. Ovid himself referred to his crime contritely as *carmen et error*, "a poem and a mistake," and believed it to be worse than murder.

Whatever the reason, Ovid died in exile, censored. But until his death in AD 18, he fought to uphold his reputation as a poet and establish his place as one of the world's literary greats. He would undoubtedly be happy to know that, more than two thousand years later, he is considered one of the wittiest and most ingenious poets of classical antiquity. He would also be gratified to know that his work and his life have inspired numerous books and plays, including novels by James Joyce, artwork by Peter Paul Rubens, music by Benjamin Britten, songs by Bob Dylan, a film by Jean Cocteau, a poem by Alexander Pushkin, and *Metamorphosis: Junior Year*, a young adult novel by Betsy Franco.